Wings

by MARY KENNEDY

pictures by
PATTI STREN

SCHOLASTIC BOOK SERVICES
NEW YORK · TORONTO · LONDON · AUCKLAND · SYDNEY · TOKYO

ISBN 0-590-31286-3

Text copyright © 1980 by Mary Kennedy. Illustrations copyright © 1980 by Patti Stren. All rights reserved. Published by Scholastic Book Services, a division of Scholastic Magazines, Inc.

12 11 10 9 8 7 6 5 4 3 2 1   4   0 1 2 3 4 5/8
                        Printed in the U.S.A.   02

for Peter Van Courtlandt Morris
with affection and gratitude
and for Carlotta and Dora, too.
                              M. Kennedy

for Dr. Kapetansky who sees a butterfly in
every caterpillar; David, my brother (and
fellow conspirator); and my mom who let
David and me keep all the moths, lizards,
frogs, toads, worms, praying mantises, hurt
birds, and garter snakes we dragged home.
And for my dad who put up with it all.
                              P. Stren

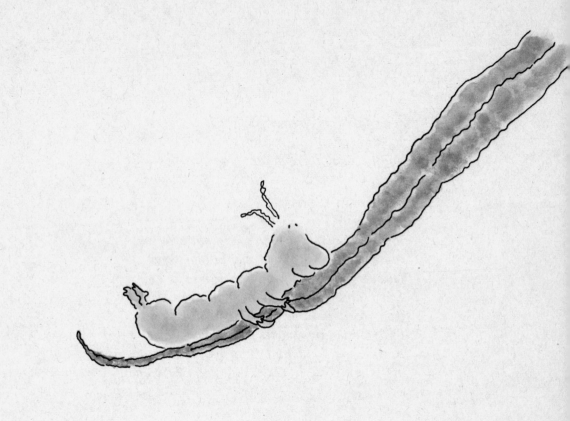

One sunny day a little caterpillar slid down
from the branch of a willow tree.

The caterpillar was hungry.
She made her way to a nearby rock
and nibbled the pink rock cress that grew there.

A young garter snake came out of the violet bed.

"What's your name?" he asked.

"Caterpillar. What's yours?"

"Garter Snake. Everybody knows me.
They admire my golden stripes
and my shining dark green skin."

May I join you?

Have a bit of cre

She stood on end and stretched.

Then she curled down softly and slowly.

"You don't do that right," said the garter snake.
"Can't you put more movement into it . . .
more wiggle and twist?

Like this."

The caterpillar tried.

"No, no, that's not it," said the snake.

"I can't quite catch that sideways swish,"
the caterpillar said.

"Try again. Watch me!" said the snake.

He did an up and over,

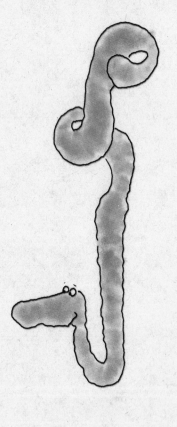

and a side to side,

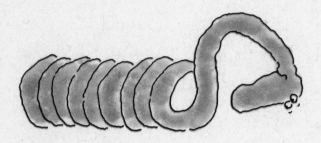

and then whirled into a circle.

"*Do that!*"

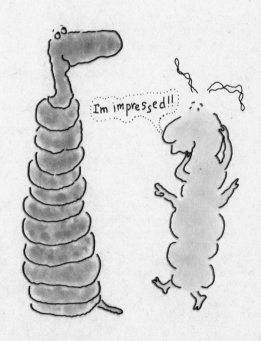

The caterpillar tried as hard as she could.
She clung to the rock with the hooks on her
short back legs. She raised her other legs
as high as possible. Then she came down
in a careful curving motion.

"How's that?" she asked, proudly.

"Terrible. You'll never be a snake!
There wasn't the slightest sidewise motion
in your dance.
Once more!"

The caterpillar stretched out on a leaf. She
turned slightly green, but she tried again.

The garter snake gazed at her sadly.
"I'm afraid you just haven't the talent."

A wren was watching from an apple tree.
"I thought she did quite well," said the wren.

"Thank you," said the caterpillar.
"But I think the snake is right.
If I could rest for a while, I might be able to learn.
Just now I want to go to sleep.
I want to sleep . . . sleep . . ."

"*Sleep?*" the garter snake said.
"If you give up like that,
you'll never amount to anything.
Oh, well, I guess we
can't all be garter snakes."

The caterpillar crawled back onto the tree.
She spun something fine and glossy and tied
herself to a branch.

"What are you doing?" the garter snake asked.

"I don't want to fall off," the caterpillar said.
She split her striped covering and wriggled out of it.

"I'll just wrap my feet up, they feel a bit cold."
The caterpillar's voice was drowsy as she made
herself comfortable.

"You're a funny one!" said the garter snake.
And he glided away to another part of the garden.
Then he forgot about the caterpillar.

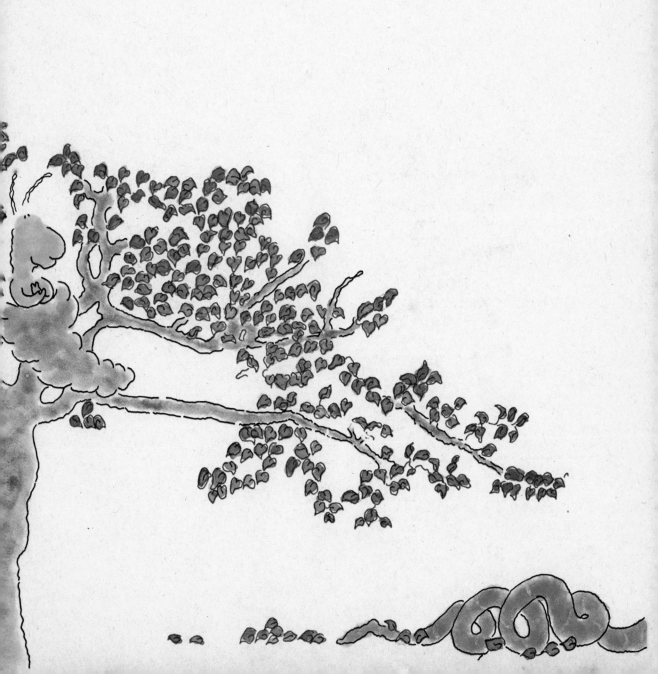

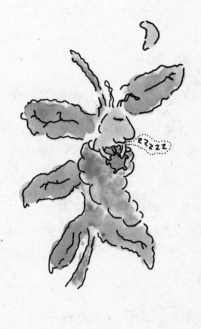

It was spring before the garter snake remembered
the caterpillar again.
"Poor little thing," he thought.
"I wonder what became of her."
And he went back to the tree to find out.

All he could see was a strange-looking bundle
hanging from the stem of a leaf.
"Caterpillar, is that you?" he called.
"My, you're a sleepyhead!
Do you know how long you've been there?"

The bundle stirred . . . it shook. Something
purple, and burning blue, with a flash of yellow,
fell out of it. Then came long thin black legs,
a little button head, eyes that looked at the
garter snake dreamily.

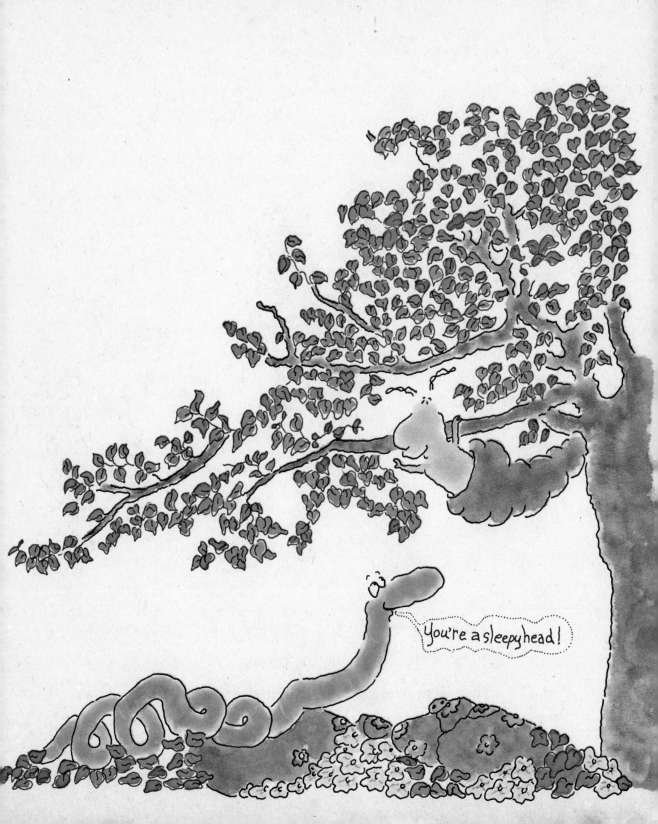

"Have I been asleep long?" she asked, stretching a
sticky wing to dry it in the air.
Then she stretched out another wing and waved it.

"WINGS!" exclaimed the garter snake. "How on earth?
Caterpillar, *what have you done?*"

The butterfly balanced herself on a narrow leaf
and fanned her wings in the breeze.

"You must call me Butterfly now," she murmured.

"Did I . . . did I say anything? Was it anything
I said that made you gorgeous like that?"

"I don't think so," the butterfly answered.
She whirled through the air in circles and spirals.

"But what did you *do*? I insist that you tell me.
I was there at the beginning of this.
I must have wings too."

"I didn't do anything," the butterfly said. "I really didn't do anything."

"Oh, think please, *think*. There must be something you can tell me. I must grow wings."

The wren looked out from her little house.
"Why aren't you happy the way you are?" she asked.
"I'm happy just to be me," she said.
And she began to sing.

"That's all right for you to say," interrupted the garter snake.
"You already have wings. There must be
something she can tell me.
Butterfly," he called. "Tell me what you did!"

"I didn't do anything, I just went to sleep."

"Oh, that must be it! Plenty of rest!
I'll go to sleep and see what happens.
If you think of anything else, I'll be under that rock
near the irises."

The garter snake slid over to the rock and yawned.
But he wasn't sleepy.

A hummingbird flew by and laughed.

"Keep quiet!" the garter snake shouted. "I'm trying to sleep.
It isn't easy." He closed his eyes.

"My poor boy," said the wren gently.

"Don't waste your time. You'll never grow wings."

"Why not?" said the little snake.

"What one can do another can do.

Why can't I grow wings?"

"Because your parents didn't have wings. That's why."

"My parents had wings," said the butterfly.

"So had mine," said the hummingbird,

"and my wife's parents had wings too."

"You mean I'll never be able to fly?"
said the garter snake. He tried not to cry.

"No, you won't," the butterfly said.
"But you dance like a dream."

"Yes, I do, don't I?" said the snake.
He did his special twist and twirl.
"There are not many as good as I am. My parents
were quite graceful too. I guess I like myself
the way I am."

The wren sang.

The butterfly fluttered.

The hummingbird gathered honey.

The sun sparkled.

And the little garter snake practiced his dancin